Billboard

by

Michael Vukadinovich

SAMUEL FRENCH

FOUNDED 1830

NEW YORK HOLLYWOOD LONDON TORONTO

SAMUELFRENCH.COM

ISBN 978-0-573-66280-5   Printed in U.S.A.   #4256

IMPORTANT BILLING AND CREDIT REQUIREMENTS

BILLBOARD was developed at the UCLA Graduate School of Theatre where it received a workshop performance.

BILLBOARD received its world premiere production in New York City by Reverie Productions and Overlap Productions on January 12, 2007 at 59E59 Theaters. It was directed by Tania Inessa Kirkman. The cast was as follows:

ANDY . . . . Ken Matthews
KATELYN . . . . Sarah K. Lippmann
DAMON . . . . Joey Piscopo

Stage Manager: Christie Love Santiago
Assistant Stage Manager: Mariana Carbonell
Sets: Zhanna Gurvich and Gaetane Bertol
Lights: Colin D. Young
Costumes: Carla Bellisio
Sound: Elizabeth Coleman
Video Designer: David Kreger
Co-Producer: Susanna L. Harris
Assoc. Producer: Anna Hayman
Graphic Design: Angela McNally
Publicity: Karen Greco

For CML

CHARACTERS

Andy
Katelyn
Damon

AUTHOR'S NOTE

When a character's line ends or begins with ellipses it implies continuous (as much as is possible) dialogue through the interruption.

"Monopoly scorns art."
 – *Theodor Adorno*

ACT ONE

Scene 1

SCENE: Los Angeles. The apartment of Andy and Kate-lyn. A small apartment with almost all second-hand furnishings. It isn't completely out of style however. There is a touch of the artist.

(KATELYN and DAMON are staring at a tattoo on ANDY's forehead. The tattoo is a set of headphones with the company name "Questa" written underneath. They sit in an awkward mix of shock and disbelief which lasts throughout the scene. KATELYN is obviously very upset. Silence.)

DAMON. Did it hurt?

ANDY. Like hell.

DAMON. Oh.

(Silence as they look at the tattoo)

It sort of looks like Japanese characters, if you squint your eyes. My cousin got a tattoo of Japanese characters on his arm. Supposedly it means courage but he doesn't know for sure.

ANDY. It's a pair of headphones, Damon. Not Japanese characters.

DAMON. They probably make their products in Asia so there could be Japanese characters. Some subliminal message that says, "Buy our shit." How would we know?

We can't read Japanese.

ANDY. Then it wouldn't matter would it?

(More silence)

DAMON. A real tattoo? What the hell were you thinking Andy?

ANDY. I can get it removed in a year.

(More silence)

ANDY. It's a lot of money for doing nothing but leaving my forehead uncovered.

DAMON. So what is it exactly? Questa? What is Questa?

ANDY. *(Mechanically)* They make MP3 and CD players. Questa's slogan is, "Questa, the sound you've been searching for."

(Beat)

Stop looking at me like that.

DAMON. You should have gotten something cool, like a cougar.

KATELYN. Of all the stupidest, idiotic things you could have possibly done behind my back. Really?

ANDY. I didn't think you'd understand…

KATELYN. IT'S A TATTOO OF A CORPORATE LOGO ON YOUR FOREHEAD.

ANDY. Yeah, but at least it's a nice looking…

KATELYN. Couldn't you have gone to a strip club or something like normal guys do when their girlfriends are out of town?

ANDY. Not sanitary. Besides, I didn't even know if I was going to do it or not until the last minute.

KATELYN. Or the first minute I wasn't there to stop you.

ANDY. It's a way to make money…

KATELYN. It's your face!

ANDY. …like any other job.

KATELYN. You're like a prostitute or something.

ANDY. I realize it isn't exactly ideal for you…

KATELYN. Ideal?…

ANDY. …but it gives us options. Upward mobility…

KATELYN. No Andy, this couldn't be any more ideal…

ANDY. We'll be able to pay our rent on time for starters.

KATELYN. …maybe next I can date Joe Camel.

ANDY. Hell, we can even get a nicer, bigger place some-where safer.

(*Pause*)

He's not used anymore.

KATELYN. What?

ANDY. Joe Camel. They stopped using him because of the kids. They were all smoking…

KATELYN. WHAT THE HELL ARE YOU TALKING ABOUT?

ANDY. …Don't be upset. I was just pointing out…

KATELYN. UPSET? WHY WOULD I BE UPSET?

ANDY. Just listen. If I stayed at the bookstore it would take over fifteen years just to pay off my…our student loans. That's without credit card debt. Don't give me that look. I have Excel sheets Katelyn. You want to see the Excel sheets…

KATELYN. This is sick…

ANDY. I learned the formulas…This is great! In what other country could I get paid so much for so little? I wish you'd understand Katelyn…

KATELYN. …And I wish you'd understand that I don't…

ANDY. …It's only for a year…

KATELYN. …want to date a GOD DAMN BILLBOARD!

ANDY. …and it will affect our future forever. Think about that. Of what we'll be able to buy. A new car, furniture, better art supplies for you. You're always complaining about how much money you need to be an artist. Well now you can be one.

KATELYN. It's humiliating…

ANDY. Sure people will stare at it but that's the damn

point.

KATELYN. …Was that your plan, to humiliate me?…

ANDY. …You think sorting books all day or catching little punks stealing porno mags isn't humiliating? Hard work is the most humiliating thing I've ever done. This is nothing.

KATELYN. *(Giving up, looking for help)* Damon?

DAMON. We're all living off credit. God knows I had to get a platinum card just to pay off my gold card which I got to pay off my car payments. Somehow you thought this was the best way to solve your problems?

ANDY. We've been friends for a very long time.

DAMON. Since my second fourth grade.

(To **KATELYN***)*

Bureaucracy.

ANDY. And I don't expect you to understand. You're an idealist with everything. Have always been an idealist.

DAMON. That's not entirely…

ANDY. …No, listen. It always has to be black and white with you. You protested Afghanistan, you protested Iraq, you protested Ralph's…

DAMON. And now I'm protesting the invasion of Andy Price's forehead.

ANDY. …Like it was all so simple.

DAMON. I don't think any of this is simple…

ANDY. The cell phone company protest?

DAMON. What about it?

ANDY. American companies made contract bids before the bombs even dropped. So what?

DAMON. …Other countries were kept from bidding.

ANDY. It was our soldiers, our weapons, our blood.

DAMON. Our? Exactly where do you fit in that our? It was just one big marketing campaign.

ANDY. So you told me. On your cell phone…

DAMON. …It's for emergencies…

ANDY. You called me from your car…

DAMON. …My mom feels safer…

ANDY. …your car… which has a "No Blood for Oil" bumper sticker. Do you not see the irony in that? I could understand if it was on your bike, sure.

KATELYN. This isn't about Damon's bike.

ANDY. It's about how everything is complicated.

KATELYN. Oh, I think this one is pretty simple, Andy.

ANDY. Sometimes you have to make sacrifices to get the life you want. I am making a sacrifice here Katelyn…

KATELYN. You don't even know what you're sacrificing Andy…

ANDY. You're looking at me like I'm crazy, but Questa is the crazy one. Paying me for nothing. The trick is on them, not the other way around.

(Triumphant)

I've swindled Questa. And for a lot of money!

KATELYN. I DON'T CARE ABOUT MONEY! We never pay our bills so why should we care about money?!

ANDY. It would be like Starbucks paying me to go around and drink coffee all day.

KATELYN. No, it would be like Starbucks paying you a lot of money to tattoo their logo on your forehead. That's what it would be like.

(More silence)

ANDY. Anyone want a beer? I'm going to get a beer.

DAMON. Yeah, I'll take one of those.

(ANDY exits into the kitchen.)

DAMON. Do you think that's ironic? A "No Blood for Oil" bumper sticker?

KATELYN. Did you really not know about this?

DAMON. I knew as much as you.

(ANDY returns drinking a beer and gives one to DAMON who also drinks.)

ANDY. You know what would be crazy? Letting economics keep me from doing what I really want to do when I can change that so easily.

KATELYN. Yes, but you're a tool…

ANDY. We're all tools.

DAMON. But we don't all have ugly tattoos on our foreheads.

ANDY. It's not that ugly…

DAMON. It's a flesh wound and you're missing the point.

ANDY. …you have to imagine it without all the dead skin.

(He begins to look at it in the mirror)

DAMON. You know who gets tattoos on their foreheads?… People like Charles Manson…

ANDY. I am nothing like…

DAMON. …goddamn Charlie fucking M. himself.

ANDY. …What?

DAMON. People like god damn Charles Manson get tattoos on their foreheads. Sure he could play the guitar, but all those murders? That's something to think about.

ANDY. Who are you?

DAMON. If Charles Manson wore Levis, I wouldn't wear Levis, let alone get a tattoo on my forehead.

ANDY. …You don't wear Levis anyway.

DAMON. No, I don't wear Levis because I don't support god damn Charles Manson.

ANDY. You don't wear Levis because you insist that they're made by six-year-old Asian children who are kept at the age of six all their lives with secret drugs produced by the CIA.

DAMON. That's not fair…I was drunk when I…

ANDY. …What's not fair is that I am being criticized by my two best friends for making a strategic business decision in order to better our lives.

KATELYN. Business decision? What do you know about business decisions?

DAMON. …Even if they're not kept at the age of six with drugs, they get new kids to replace them when they turn seven…That was my point…

ANDY. Companies pay a lot of money to advertise their products on our televisions, buses, newspapers, in our schools.

KATELYN. Yes, but not on the students!

DAMON. …Think about that, retiring at seven.

ANDY. Do you want to know how much money I'm making…

KATELYN. No, I don't want to know.

ANDY. Well you know how much debt I'm in because of college. And it's not like an English degree is exactly lucrative. Plus I haven't even had time to write because I've had to work so much. Well, I don't have to worry about that anymore.

KATELYN. Don't tell me you quit your job.

ANDY. What's the point of working when there's money to be made?

KATELYN. Jesus, Andy.

ANDY. When we get the check, you'll see it differently. This is like winning the lottery.

DAMON. Once your book is published you can advertise it on your nose.

ANDY. *(Serious)* I'm forbidden from selling anymore ad space on my body. Contractual agreement.

DAMON. You're losing what little sense of humor you had.

KATELYN. Now when people ask I can say my boyfriend works in marketing.

ANDY. *(Correcting)* Guerilla advertising.

DAMON. We all have to work Andy.

ANDY. Yes, but you like working at the record store. You're happy there. It's your thing. Plus you live with your mom for free.

DAMON. You know why I live at home.

ANDY. I'm just pointing it out. And Katelyn works at the gallery and god knows Pamela Sweeney doesn't pay.

KATELYN. It's an internship, Andy. It's about experience.

ANDY. It doesn't help with the bills. That's my point. Now let's just drop this for now.

(The following dialogue is awkward as **ANDY** *attempts to divert attention from the tattoo. To* **KATELYN***)*

I want to know about your trip. Tell me about your trip.

(To **DAMON***)*

Thanks for picking her up from the airport. My car is...

DAMON. ...Dead. I know.

ANDY. And LA is such...

DAMON. ...A horrible city to be without a car.

ANDY. Thanks.

DAMON. No problem.

ANDY. So did everything go okay?

... The funeral?

KATELYN. It was... well it was fine.

I mean it sucked, but it was fine.

I didn't really know my Uncle, but these things always...

ANDY. ...I know. But I'm glad you're home.

(Kisses her, she doesn't respond)

I couldn't hear a thing when I called you. No reception at all. How horrible it is when you say I love you and the person on the other end shouts back "what?"

Well guess what I did yesterday?

I went to the Zoo.

Who knew LA had a zoo?

DAMON. How did you get there?

ANDY. I took the bus.

It was really depressing.

The zoo, not the bus.

Well both actually. I mean it isn't even a very nice zoo.
The cages are too small and all the animals just look
sedated.

DAMON. I protested against that zoo once.

ANDY. I don't think I'll go back. Who really needs to go to
the zoo anymore with television…

KATELYN. …YOU HAVE A TATTOO ON YOUR FORE-
HEAD!…

ANDY. Katelyn don't…

KATELYN. …And you want to talk about animals at the zoo?
Didn't you think of me AT ALL?

ANDY. I did it for you.

KATELYN. Well thank you Andy Price. What more could a
girl want? And in my favorite color too! How did you
know?

ANDY. Katelyn, you're being…

KATELYN. What? I'm being what?

ANDY. Unreasonable.

KATELYN. I can't be reasonable with you anymore.

DAMON. Maybe Damon should leave.

KATELYN. Then I'm going with you.

ANDY. Stay Damon. Everything is fine. You're my two…

KATELYN. No, I think I am going to go.

ANDY. …best friends. Just stay.

KATELYN. For some reason I have the sudden urge to go
buy a new GODDAMN MP3 PLAYER.

(*Begins to exit*)

ANDY. Wait. Katelyn. I did it because I wanted to buy you a
ring. An engagement ring.

(**KATELYN** *stops, long silence*)

Scene 2

*(**ANDY** is alone and has a camera hanging around his neck.)*

ANDY. *(To the audience)* An excerpt from years ago. It's raining hard.

(Rain sounds are heard)

Katelyn and I stayed in bed all day and decided to listen to every Beatles album in order.

*(**KATELYN** appears lying in bed under the covers, apparently naked. **ANDY** walks to her, takes off his shirt, and gets in the bed. The Beatles play softly.)*

We talked about our favorite albums.

KATELYN. Magical Mystery Tour. Everyone says Sgt. Peppers is so progressive, but Magical Mystery Tour was just as ahead of its time.

ANDY. *(To **KATELYN**)* Come on, Abbey Road by far.

(He takes her picture.)

KATELYN. *(Playfully)* I told you to stop that. I look gross.

ANDY. You can tell by listening to that album they're about to break up. By far their best. John or Paul?

KATELYN. George.

ANDY. Not fair. Long hair or short?

KATELYN. Medium.

(He takes her picture again.)

Hey!

ANDY. Well if you'd answer my questions properly.

KATELYN. I will. I promise.

ANDY. Best post-Beatle?

KATELYN. Ringo.

ANDY. What?

KATELYN. Kidding. John.

ANDY. And your favorite song?

KATELYN. Julia. I'm going to name my daughter after that song.

ANDY. How many of those are you going to have?

KATELYN. Children? Two. A boy and a girl.

ANDY. You seem pretty sure of that. And the boy's name?

KATELYN. Thor.

ANDY. I hope you have girls. Where do you want to live?

KATELYN. Anywhere walking distance from the ocean. In a house though, not an apartment. I've never lived in a house.

ANDY. Sounds expensive.

KATELYN. There's a story by Salinger where he describes how it would be nice if every house looked identical so that people would come home to the wrong house, eat dinner with the wrong family by mistake, sleep in the wrong bed and kiss everybody goodbye in the morning thinking they were your own family. I always thought that was nice.

ANDY. If every house looked the same I might never see you again.

KATELYN. But it's nice to think of everyone going home to the wrong house and nobody caring.

ANDY. Profession?

KATELYN. Ideally a painter. Realistically, maybe work at a museum. A curator or something.

ANDY. Well you're the best painter I know.

KATELYN. You'll probably be the only person who'll ever buy my work, and that won't help us any. And even if I did have the talent, I don't have the money. What about you?

ANDY. Marry rich. Smile.

(*He takes her picture again, she doesn't protest.*)

Car?

KATELYN. A Volkswagen Bug. But not one of the new ones. I want an old one.

ANDY. Color?

KATELYN. Orange.

ANDY. Pets?

KATELYN. Dogs. Beagles maybe.

ANDY. Big wedding?

KATELYN. Smallish.

ANDY. In a church?

KATELYN. Yes, but not by a priest.

ANDY. And are you going to wear white?

KATELYN. It's not called a white lie for nothing.

ANDY. Time of year?

KATELYN. Fall.

ANDY. Honeymoon?

KATELYN. Africa.

ANDY. Africa?

KATELYN. I like animals.

ANDY. How long before children?

KATELYN. Three years.

(Takes her picture)

ANDY. In between children?

KATELYN. Two.

ANDY. Would you take your husband's last name?

(He goes under the covers.)

KATELYN. Hyphenate.

ANDY. Ideal proposal?

(Takes a picture of her under the covers.)

KATELYN. Unexpected. On one knee.

ANDY. You do like your men on their knees.

KATELYN. I like to bring them there.

(He takes another picture of her under the covers.)

I'm supposed to be the artist here.

ANDY. But you're such a sexy model. Religion?

KATELYN. On holidays in small doses. For the kids.

ANDY. Close to your mother in law?

KATELYN. On holidays in small doses. For the kids.

(He takes another picture.)

ANDY. Second honeymoon?

KATELYN. Paris.

ANDY. *(Sticking his head out from under the covers)* Expensive taste.

KATELYN. *(In a French accent, playfully)* Not expensive. Refined my friend.

ANDY. Ideal death?

KATELYN. Old. In my bed. You?

ANDY. Young, in someone else's bed.

KATELYN. Do you really think we'll last?

(He takes another picture of her, gets out of the bed and begins to put his shirt back on, then to the audience:)

ANDY. And she continued to paint me the whole picture of her future and I was in the middle of it. And the picture was a good one, and I wanted to give it to her, but I had none of the brushes.

*(**KATELYN** gets up and takes the camera from him. Enter **DAMON** with a recorder. **ANDY** is now being interviewed and the interviewers are played by **KATELYN** and **DAMON**. **ANDY** dresses as the interview takes place. **KATELYN** flirts with him and takes his picture throughout the scene.)*

INTERVIEWER/DAMON. Tell us, Andy, what exactly is the deal you made with Questa and why.

INTERVIEWER/KATELYN. What was the reasoning behind such an extreme decision?

ANDY. For me it's about using the system to make a better life for me and my girlfriend. I did it for her.

INTERVIEWER/KATELYN. That's sweet. That you'd make such a sacrifice.

ANDY. I'm just taking advantage of what's out there. You don't achieve the American dream by sleeping. You have to make it happen. And for Questa, it's about making an impact. People see on average three- to four-thousand ads a day. Think about that. And how many of those ads do people actually remember? Advertisers are always looking for new ways to get through. People remember the weird. Talk about the unusual. That's how this idea arose.

INTERVIEWER/DAMON. How savvy of you to realize all of this.

ANDY. I saw Questa's ad in the paper and I figured why not take advantage of this opportunity? I have Excel sheets detailing how to most effectively alleviate my debt.

INTERVIEWER/KATELYN. Excel. How impressive.

ANDY. I know all the formulas. Well, most. So now all I have to do is go around and do my thing and Questa's name is plastered right on my head.

INTERVIEWER/DAMON. Do you think this type of advertising will last?

INTERVIEWER/KATELYN. Is this just a short term fad or a new phenomenon? Is Andy Price the new mold for marketing firms?

ANDY. I don't know how long this will last but it seems to be catching on. I've never been interviewed in the paper before, or on TV, and now people are calling from around the world asking me questions, setting up interviews and photo shoots. Someone called me from Helsinki the other day to ask me some questions for a Finnish magazine.

INTERVIEWER/KATELYN. Finland? How exotic!

ANDY. I had to look it up on a map. What a kick. People want to take pictures with me or tell me congratulations when I walk down the street. They call me Questa Man. I don't know if this will last or if it's a new phenomenon but I know it's great for me.

INTERVIEWER/KATELYN. Do you ever find it embarrassing or wish you hadn't done it?

INTERVIEWER/DAMON. There must be moments of regret.

ANDY. Sure there are things you don't think about. But no, I don't regret it. You always hear celebrities complaining about fame, but it's great! And besides, this isn't a risk for me.

INTERVIEWER/KATELYN. Have you had any negative reaction to the tattoo?

ANDY. Sure some people think I'm an idiot, but I just say to each their own. My girlfriend Katelyn wasn't exactly thrilled when I came home with the tattoo.

INTERVIEWER/KATELYN. You mean, she didn't know you were going to do this?

ANDY. Well, no, but I did it for her. She's a really great artist and as soon as I get the check, I'm going to buy her all new supplies.

INTERVIEWER/KATELYN. That's so thoughtful of you. It must be hard for you, her not realizing why you did this.

ANDY. She'll come around. She's just a little…surprised.

INTERVIEWER/DAMON. What else do you plan to do with the money?

ANDY. I'm going to spend it! First, I'm going to pay off my bills and loans and then I'm just going to sit back and not worry about a thing.

INTERVIEWER/DAMON. Will you do this type of thing again?

INTERVIEWER/KATELYN. What's next for Andy Price?

ANDY. I've been thinking about new things and I've had other companies approach me with ideas. I've opened a door for myself with this and I need to get through before it shuts.

INTERVIEWER/DAMON. What sort of ideas?

ANDY. I can't say right now but I promise they'll be good.

INTERVIEWER/DAMON. Congratulations on your business decision.

INTERVIEWER/KATELYN. On your initiative.

(**DAMON** *moves to the side as if presenting him to the audience,* **KATELYN** *kneels in front of him for a picture.*)

INTERVIEWER/KATELYN. The Human Commercial!

INTERVIEWER/DAMON. The Walking Billboard!

(**KATELYN** *takes* **ANDY**'s *picture*)

Scene 3

*(Now late at night. **KATELYN** enters from the bedroom very upset. She is in her pajamas. She sits down on the couch and begins flipping through a magazine. After a moment **ANDY** enters putting on his shirt.)*

ANDY. What did…

KATELYN. You didn't even realize?

ANDY. …I do?

KATELYN. Think Andy. Think of what you said?

ANDY. I wasn't saying…

KATELYN. Think.

ANDY. …anything.

KATELYN. No, you said something.

ANDY. What could I have possibly said? I never say anything. You always make fun of me for how quiet I am.

KATELYN. Think, Andy.

ANDY. I said…

KATELYN. Think!

ANDY. …your name. I said your name.

KATELYN. YOU SAID A NAME!

ANDY. What? I said your…

KATELYN. IT WASN'T my name Andy.

ANDY. That's crazy. Whose name would I have said?

KATELYN. Think!

ANDY. There's no way. You're the only…

KATELYN. …one in your bed so you think you would have gotten it right.

ANDY. Whose name could I have said? You probably heard wrong…

KATELYN. I have twenty-twenty hearing!

ANDY. …you were being sort of loud yourself. That's eye sight.

KATELYN. Don't give yourself credit for that. Sounds can be deceiving.

ANDY. Just tell me what I said.

KATELYN. I was lying there Andy, with you on top, and all I could see was Questa. The Questa logo coming at me and then away, at me and then away, at me and then away. And then you said it. I can't believe you said it.

ANDY. What did I say?

KATELYN. QUESTA. You said Questa!

ANDY. What? No. No. I said Katelyn. You must have been looking at the logo and then just thought I said Questa. Some sort of transference or projecting or something. They sound similar. Katelyn. Questa.

KATELYN. I know what I heard. You called me Questa. And you didn't even realize it.

ANDY. Why would I say Questa? This is crazy.

KATELYN. You tell me why you said it. I mean, I've heard of being fucked by big business, but this is too much.

ANDY. Listen to me, I didn't say Katelyn. I mean Questa. I said Katelyn and not Questa.

KATELYN. See.

ANDY. Katelyn, don't.

KATELYN. How could you have said…

ANDY. …I didn't.

(Silence)

Fine, let's say for a minute that I actually said Questa. So what? It's not like I said some other girl's name or something. All it means is that I got the words mixed up in my head. If I even said it.

KATELYN. You did.

ANDY. I don't think I did.

KATELYN. YOU SAID IT.

ANDY. Do you think I'm cheating on you with Questa? Is that it. You caught me, Katelyn. I admit it. I am cheating on you WITH A WHOLE CORPORATE COMPANY. Yes, I've slept with all 10,000 employees.

KATELYN. Stop. Andy.

ANDY. I didn't mean for this to happen.

KATELYN. Stop acting!

ANDY. It's funny. They're a lot like you.

KATELYN. You're being absurd!

ANDY. This whole thing is absurd.

KATELYN. Why would you say it? At such a moment?

ANDY. I didn't say it.

KATELYN. Do you think I imagined it?

ANDY. I can't control your imagination, Katelyn.

KATELYN. How would you feel if I just shouted out Wal-Mart?

ANDY. Are you really asking me this?

KATELYN. ...Or Apple?...

ANDY. Look, Katelyn...

KATELYN. ...Or Pepsi? Oh Apple! Kiss me Wal-Mart. Do me Google!

ANDY. Stop! You know why I did this.

KATELYN. It's like you have to marry someone else before you can marry me.

ANDY. I'm doing it so I can marry you. I'm making it possible.

KATELYN. Maybe you didn't say Questa. Maybe it was my imagination but just the fact that I would imagine it is enough.

ANDY. In the morning you'll probably think this whole conversation is stupid. Isn't that what always happens when you get like this? You'll get up early. Make the coffee. We'll have that awkward first eye contact and nothing will have to be said. Understood, but not said. And we'll drink coffee.

Scene 4

(KATELYN is alone. She is painting at an easel which the audience cannot see the front of.)

KATELYN. *(To the audience)* On the plane I sat next to this little girl and her mother. The little girl was drawing with crayons for most of the trip. Pictures of her house and family and pets. Drawings from a child's mind. Every once in awhile she would start drawing on the plane, either on the window or the tray, wherever. And her mom would say to her, "Stop drawing on the plane honey. If you can't stay between the lines at least stay on the paper.'

After awhile I noticed that every time the plane dipped or there was a bit of turbulence she would begin to draw on it. I think it was because she wanted to control the plane. That she thought if she could somehow make it part of her drawing, part of the world she knew, then she would be safe. When you draw something you seem to somehow understand it better.

When I was a little girl, about six or seven – the same as the girl on the plane – I was having bad dreams every night. My parents, both struggling artists, finally decided to pay and send me to a psychiatrist because they were so tired from me sleeping in their bed. The first thing the psychiatrist had me do was draw my nightmares out on paper with crayons. Simply draw my dreams. All the frightening images I had seen the night before in the darkness of sleep.

Telling someone your dreams is one thing, but to draw them another. The difference between Freud and Picasso. Those monsters and creatures that made me so scared in bed the night before looked so cartoonish and ridiculous when I drew them out and explained them to her. They were exposed. Out of their darkness. In the light. After only about three or four visits my nightmares stopped completely. They moved from my head to the paper and they were filed away in a cabinet forever. A few years later, after my father died, I began to draw again. This time for myself.

(ANDY and DAMON enter as KATELYN exits. They stare at the painting. DAMON looks at it for several moments, switching angles often.)

DAMON. *(after some contemplation of the painting)* It's… it's…

ANDY. I know.

(long silence, more examining)

DAMON. I'm no art critic but…

ANDY. I look horrible.

DAMON. It's not exactly flattering and it is certainly you, but there's a certain…profundity here. The color, the shadowing. This is good.

ANDY. This isn't good.

DAMON. When did she paint this?

ANDY. Last night. We had a…fight of sorts and she wouldn't come back to bed. She stayed up and painted and when I woke up this morning this was here and she was gone. All she's been doing is working at the gallery preparing for some new exhibit. She works for free and then criticizes me for getting this?

DAMON. I wish I had a portrait of myself.

ANDY. I look like a freak!

DAMON. I really think that this is something that could sell. People are always paying way too much for art like this.

(Silence as they look at it)

What do you think it means?

ANDY. I don't have a clue.

(More silence)

DAMON. I'd say she's pissed.

ANDY. I knew she was upset, angry even, but I wasn't expecting this.

DAMON. Pissed like a donkey.

ANDY. Look at the colors. The reds and yellows on the side and the black and blue on the other.

DAMON. Yeah, there's a duality to it. It's an obvious representation of her menstrual cycle and how it changes her perception of you.

ANDY. It doesn't represent her…can we not talk about my girlfriend's period.

DAMON. Don't be such a prude. It's the cycle of life, man.

ANDY. It's not the actual menstrual cycle that I mind, it's hearing you talk about it that's making me feel sick.

DAMON. Regardless, you're fucked.

ANDY. Why?

DAMON. You had to go and get a talented girlfriend and now you're paying the price.

ANDY. And what price am I paying Damon?

DAMON. Your girlfriend, fiancee, whatever, is amazingly talented. Why would she stay with an ass with a tattoo on his forehead like Charles Manson?

ANDY. I told you to stop with the Charles Manson thing.

DAMON. Secondly, men never stay with talented women.

ANDY. That's ridiculous…

DAMON. …It's true. We can't handle it. Women make us feel inadequate enough. We don't need their talent emasculating us too.

ANDY. That is the stupidest theory you've put forth yet.

DAMON. Joan of Arc, Gertrude Stein.

ANDY. What about them?

DAMON. They never married.

ANDY. Those are the two worst examples you could have possibly come up with. Even if you had time, days, to think of worse examples, you wouldn't be able to do it.

DAMON. They had loads of talent.

ANDY. Gertrude Stein was a lesbian.

DAMON. And I'll bet she was a talented one.

ANDY. And Joan of Arc was burned at the stake when she was like 17.

DAMON. My point is that even if Joan of Arc were alive today, I couldn't have a relationship with her because she was too talented, talking to god and shit. I would never even be able to gather the courage to ask her out on a date.

ANDY. Damon, we are not going to break up. I have always known Katelyn is talented...

DAMON. You should have found a slow girl, Andy.

ANDY. IN FACT, that's why I was attracted to her in the first place.

DAMON. Nope.

ANDY. What do you mean *nope?*

DAMON. You were attracted to her because she is hot and I am willing to bet you were mildly annoyed when you discovered she is talented.

ANDY. That is one-hundred-percent not true.

DAMON. Women, on the other hand, are attracted to talent. Looks come in a distant second place. Third even.

ANDY. Suddenly you're an art critic and a connoisseur of women?

DAMON. Over fifty-percent of models date musicians. Ugly musicians.

ANDY. You always do this...

DAMON. You could be the ugliest man alive...

ANDY. ...You make shit up.

DAMON. ...But if you play guitar it doesn't matter to women.

ANDY. You make up facts, quotes, numbers...

DAMON. It's because women are the ones who have the kids.

ANDY. ...Statistics. Always with the statistics and percentages.

DAMON. Their ovaries tell them that talent is good. And yours would too if you had to push a kid from your loins.

ANDY. Anything to prove your point. What?

(Pause)

DAMON. Sixty-five percent of statistics are made up Andy.

(Pause)

ANDY. That doesn't even make sense.

DAMON. Of course it makes sense. They did these experiments in the seventies Andy...don't look at me like that. They did these experiments where they paired up goldfish with monkeys and gave each pair a different puzzle.

ANDY. Just stop now.

DAMON. It illustrates my point perfectly.

ANDY. I don't care.

DAMON. Well I'm not the monkey in all of this. You are. And you made the puzzle yourself, so my advice: let Katelyn be your goldfish. That's my point.

ANDY. And my point is not how well she painted me but HOW she painted me. My girlfriend is the Alanis Morissette of art

DAMON. "Jagged Little Pill" was a phenomenal album Andy. One of the best sellers of all time. It was her breakthrough. And this could be Katelyn's breakthrough. Angry woman art about the men who make them angry. Genius.

ANDY. Yes, because that's what we need, more manic art.

DAMON. Womanic, Andy. Womanic.

ANDY. Dear god.

DAMON. Well you may not like it but you have to admit this is good.

ANDY. You're being a bit effusive. I look like a...

DAMON. ...SEE, you're already having difficulty accepting Katelyn's talent.

ANDY. I am not having...

DAMON. For someone her age...

ANDY. ...Difficulty with anything.

DAMON. ...To do something this good. Two things happen in a relationship when one partner does something exceptional.

ANDY. Here we go again.

DAMON. Either your petty jealousy will cause you to act out for attention...

ANDY. Is that fifty-percent of the time?

DAMON. ...OR she will want someone else who has done something exceptional. Most likely a musician. So you better dust off your Oboe.

ANDY. Saxophone. I played the saxophone. And anyway, I didn't have you come over to criticize my relationship with Katelyn.

DAMON. I'm not criticizing your relationship. I just want you to see what's going on here. Think about it. Katelyn is an artist. And you're a billboard. Now take a struggling artist. Someone like Katelyn who wants to create great art like this. What would be the lowest thing as an artist she could do? I'll tell you. PAINT A BILLBOARD.

ANDY. Damon, this is ridiculous.

(He begins to look at his tattoo in the mirror.)

DAMON. It would be like you writing advertising copy for iPods. Art and advertising, capitalism, whatever, do not go together.

ANDY. You don't think capitalism goes with anything.

DAMON. What did you fight about?

ANDY. What?

DAMON. You said you fought last night. What did you fight about?

ANDY. It was nothing.

DAMON. Obviously it was something.

ANDY. *(Somewhat embarrassed)* She thought I said Questa instead of Katelyn when we were...you know.

DAMON. Did you?

ANDY. Of course not. I don't think so.

DAMON. Women always hear what they don't want to hear.

ANDY. You sure know a lot for someone who's never had a serious girlfriend.

DAMON. That's not true…

ANDY. Who?

DAMON. Jennifer Neeson.

ANDY. She was…

DAMON. …TALENTED. It didn't work out.

ANDY. I was going to say underage.

DAMON. I didn't know at the time.

ANDY. You went to her prom. I have the picture.

DAMON. We were talking about the painting.

ANDY. I went with you to rent your tux.

DAMON. I think Katelyn's point here, since you're tying to figure this out, is that since the tattoo, her perception of you has shifted.

ANDY. It's just a little ink injected under the skin…

DAMON. It's a symbol.

ANDY. …That can be easily removed with lasers.

DAMON. A tattoo is a symbol of who you are. It identifies you as a person. Primitive tribes, Andy,…

ANDY. Oh Jesus.

DAMON. …PRIMITIVE tribes used tattoos as means of identification for when the spirit left the body and traveled to the next world. It was something sacred.

ANDY. Now you're an expert on tattoos?! It's on the outside. It's like the cliche. You can't judge a book by its…

DAMON. …CONTENTS. In our world you can't judge a book by its contents. This is good Andy and you better let her know how good it is.

Scene 5

(**DAMON** *alone, to the audience.*)

DAMON. The first time I met Katelyn was at my dad's funeral five years ago. Andy waited weeks before he introduced me to her. That's how I knew it was serious. The girls he didn't care about he'd let me meet right away. It was an unusual first meeting of course, but the thing was that while I was feeling awful about my dad, she was the only one who said anything to me that made me feel any better. Here, my friend's new girlfriend, made me feel better than any of my family or friends with just a few words. Sometimes a stranger can do so much more for us than those close to us.

After my dad's death I was especially worried about my mom because she didn't cry. It wasn't a sudden death, my father was sick for some time, but I still thought she should be crying. Later, after I moved back home, Katelyn gave me a small painting. There was no real image in the painting. Just shape and color. I liked it so I hung it in our living room. When my mom walked in she looked at it and immediately burst into tears. I don't know what she saw in it but the affect was immediate and in a way I don't understand it helped her.

Without Andy and Katelyn I don't think I would have dealt with any of it very well. Sometimes when I imagine my own funeral – I'll probably die of cancer because everyone dies of cancer – I think how cool it would be if everyone brought paint and wrote messages and drew pictures all over my casket like kids do on their friend's casts after they break a bone. They could write stories or draw memories and it might help people cry. How absurd that we need help crying! But the tears would mix with the paint and the result might be amazing.

Scene 6

(**ANDY** *and* **KATELYN** *sit on the couch eating McDonalds. After a moment:*)

KATELYN. I'm going to put it in the show.

ANDY. What? You can't put this one in.

KATELYN. I only get to put one piece in and this is by far my best work.

ANDY. What about the flower one? I like the flower one. It's my favorite.

KATELYN. This is a great opportunity for me, Andy.

ANDY. Exactly. And people like flowers. They don't want to look at me.

KATELYN. How many people my age get to be included in such a high profile show? I'm going to show my best piece.

ANDY. Pamela's only including you because you work for free.

KATELYN. Thanks, Andy. That's sweet.

ANDY. I didn't mean…Katelyn, I'm just saying. I don't think it's decent.

KATELYN. Oh, really? Well please explain to me how it's indecent.

ANDY. Well…to have everyone look at a painting which so obviously represents your…menstrual cycle.

KATELYN. You're beginning to sound like Damon. Please explain to me how this represents my menstrual cycle.

ANDY. You use a lot of red.

KATELYN. My god, Andy, you're genius. You've just opened up a whole new area of art criticism. It could be the subject of books, volumes even. I should tell Pamela Sweeney right away.

ANDY. I get it Katelyn.

KATELYN. Regardless, she's anxious to see the work. I told her about it today.

ANDY. You can't let them hang this in a gallery.

KATELYN. It's my painting…

ANDY. It's me…

KATELYN. …And I can do what I want with it.

ANDY. I'm not going to let this caricature of me hang in some gallery for anyone to see. That's what it is, a caricature.

KATELYN. Why are you being so weird about this? It's good.

ANDY. It's good where it is.

KATELYN. That is completely unfair…

ANDY. This is too personal.

KATELYN. What do you think art is?

ANDY. It isn't right for you to sell a painting of me which I don't approve of.

KATELYN. I think the needle went a little too far into your head.

ANDY. It isn't ethical.

KATELYN. You sold your forehead and you want to talk about what is ethical?

ANDY. Yes, but it is MY forehead.

KATELYN. And it is MY painting.

ANDY. Of me and MY forehead.

KATELYN. Of MY perception.

ANDY. You really want to sell this?

KATELYN. This is the best work I've ever done. By far. Besides, if someone buys it it'll be for a lot of money. Isn't that what you live for, money?

ANDY. That isn't what I live for.

KATELYN. You're willing to tattoo your forehead for money, but me selling a portrait of you is somehow unethical?

ANDY. Yes! I did this for you, and now you want people to laugh at me by turning me into a cartoon.

KATELYN. People will laugh at you regardless.

ANDY. I wouldn't share this about you…

KATELYN. This isn't even personal…I don't understand.

ANDY. And I have plenty of things about you I could share.

KATELYN. ...You wear this on your forehead for everyone to gawk and laugh at and you're worried about people laughing at a portrait? There is nothing you could say that will change my mind.

ANDY. I'm sure there's something.

KATELYN. I am an artist before I am Andy's girlfriend. I mean that.

ANDY. Five years in a relationship gives you a lot of ammunition, Katelyn.

KATELYN. Like what, Andy? Are you going to share my secrets? Is that how childish and petty this has become?

ANDY. Just think of the pictures I have of you. You wouldn't want me sharing those with anyone. And I'm sure I could find plenty of people who'd be interested. That's how I feel about this.

(A pause)

KATELYN. That is entirely different.

ANDY. Why? You have a picture of me I don't want anyone to see and I have the same of you. And we're both willing to sell.

KATELYN. How can you compare...I don't believe this. You may not have seen any value in your own body, Andy, but you better damn well see the value in mine.

ANDY. I am trying to make a point...

KATELYN. SHUT UP! You have no fucking point. All you've been doing lately is trying to make points you don't have. But this...my God...that was special. Is nothing sacred to you anymore?

ANDY. I shouldn't have...but that's what this is like...

KATELYN. YOU SHOULDN'T HAVE done any of this.

ANDY. I wasn't using my head.

KATELYN. How funny that sounds now. "Not using my head." Well don't worry about me showing it because I won't. I refuse to. But don't you dare think I'm not showing it because of you. I thought it was good. I thought I had captured something here. But I was way off. I didn't capture you at all. Not even close. It isn't nearly nasty enough. Not nearly dark enough. Much too human. In fact, it doesn't even look like you. There's been an airbrushing. Well thank you for proving me wrong! I can't even talk to you with that thing on your head.

(She storms off into the bedroom slamming the door. **ANDY** *slumps down on the couch. He then looks at the painting for a moment, gets up, looks at it again, this time really considering it. He touches his forehead and then the painting.)*

ANDY. I don't look like this.

(He picks it up and places it in the closet. He sits back down on the couch. **DAMON** *and* **KATELYN** *enter as the interviewers.* **KATELYN** *is now cold to him.)*

INTERVIEWER/DAMON. Andy Price who has come to be known as the Human Billboard after selling his forehead as add space to the Questa electronics company.

INTERVIEWER/KATELYN. The Walking Billboard who agreed to display the Questa logo on his forehead for one year.

INTERVIEWER/DAMON. Do you feel that you've been exploited here at all?

INTERVIEWER/KATELYN. You said yourself you've felt deep moments of regret.

ANDY. I never said that.

INTERVIEWER/DAMON. But you must.

INTERVIEWER/KATELYN. You have a tattoo on your forehead.

INTERVIEWER/DAMON. Surely it has changed your life greatly.

INTERVIEWER/KATELYN. People must stare.

INTERVIEWER/DAMON. Or try to not stare.

INTERVIEWER/KATELYN. Which is worse than staring.

INTERVIEWER/DAMON. Aren't you embarrassed going out? Dinners? Meetings? Seeing casual friends? Jogging?

INTERVIEWER/KATELYN. What about those around you? Your friends, family, girlfriend? Is she still around?

ANDY. Of course she's still around. Why wouldn't she still be around?

INTERVIEWER/KATELYN. But she didn't know you were going to do it.

ANDY. She didn't know I was going to propose to her either.

INTERVIEWER/DAMON. And as I recall she didn't say yes.

INTERVIEWER/KATELYN. This can't be easy for her. What you did was extreme. So irreversible.

ANDY. I can get it removed! I've felt from the beginning that I'm the one exploiting Questa. They're paying me to do nothing.

INTERVIEWER/DAMON. But you are doing something for them.

INTERVIEWER/KATELYN. They're making money off you and you have made certain sacrifices for them.

ANDY. *(doubting himself)* Yes, they're making money off me and I'm making money off them. That's work. I get paid, their sales go up. I get to go on television, their name is spread. They are getting more from me than from an entire marketing team. And I'm getting paid like it.

INTERVIEWER/DAMON. But don't you think the fact that you are getting paid for this says something negative about our culture?

INTERVIEWER/KATELYN. The extent to which we exploit the human body.

INTERVIEWER/DAMON. The objectification of the individual.

ANDY. Sure it says something about our culture. It shows how hypocritical it is. See you're no different than me in the end.

INTERVIEWER/KATELYN. We don't have tattoos on our foreheads Andy.

ANDY. Yes but you're here covering a story you may think is morally wrong for one reason: money. You think I'll be ratings for you. So just like me you're making money off this tattoo.

It's all a game. You want to criticize me but you also want things like this to happen.

INTERVIEWER/DAMON. And what really is happening Andy?

INTERVIEWER/KATELYN. Calls from Helsinki? Deals from companies?

INTERVIEWER/DAMON. Fame is great? Questa Man? Is that really what you thought you'd be saying?

ANDY. Okay. Stop!

INTERVIEWER/KATELYN. Can I take a picture with you Questa Man?

INTERVIEWER/DAMON. You've opened a door for yourself and you better get through before it shuts.

ANDY. Stop!

(He attempts to rub the tattoo off. **DAMON** *and* **KATELYN** *present him to the audience.)*

INTERVIEWER/KATELYN. The Human Commercial.

INTERVIEWER/DAMON. The Walking Billboard.

ANDY. Okay, stop!

(Black.)

End of Act One

(During intermission commercials are projected onto the stage. It is a commercial break.)

ACT TWO

Scene 1

SCENE: *The same as Act One.*

KATELYN. *(Alone, to the audience)* A fable:

A young man snuck into a museum after it was closed with a can of spray paint.

*(Enter **DAMON** with a spray paint can. **ANDY** enters from the opposite side. He is the painting and wears a frame around his head.)*

He walked up to a painting he was determined should be destroyed because he was convinced it was offensive garbage and had no right hanging in a museum of art. He was about to destroy the painting when the painting said:

ANDY. Why do you want to destroy me? I am only a mirror to your face.

KATELYN. And the man replied:

DAMON. Because you are not art. You are vulgar and dirty and should not be hanging in a museum.

ANDY. What color paint do you have?

KATELYN. ...Asked the painting.

DAMON. Red.

KATELYN. ...Said the man.

ANDY. Well if you must spray me please only spray me where I tell you. I'd hate to get paint in my eyes and mouth.

KATELYN. The man agreed because he was used to following orders and believing whatever others told him. He was a very simple man and as a result was a very popular politician. He began to spray the painting with the red paint, being careful to only spray where the painting said.

(**DAMON** *sprays the paint on* **ANDY.**)

In the end, the painting said:

ANDY. I am not nearly destroyed enough. My vulgarity still shows through. You should come back with more cans of paint. Bring blues, greens, browns and yellows.

(**DAMON** *exits.*)

KATELYN. The man agreed and came back in an hour with many more cans of paint. This time even more determined to destroy the painting.

(**DAMON** *enters with more cans of spray paint.*)

The man began to spray the painting crazily and the painting reminded him:

ANDY. Only spray where I tell you.

KATELYN. And the man agreed. He sprayed over the painting for sometime when at last the painting told him to stop. The man did, took a step back and was shocked to find that he had transformed the painting that he thought was so vulgar and disturbing into something that he now thought was so beautiful.

DAMON. What have I done?

KATELYN. …Asked the man.

ANDY. In trying to destroy me you only made me beautiful.

KATELYN. …Said the painting.

ANDY. But why haven't you done the same outside the museum? I am only the mirror…

KATELYN. …Said the painting.

The end.

(*She takes the frame off of* **ANDY,** *sets it down, and then to the audience:*)

And I said fine. If Andy is willing to blackmail me to keep me from showing his portrait, I won't show it. But there is something interesting here. More than a painting can capture. This can be turned around on him.

I can make him see what he has done. I will put the mirror to his face.

ANDY. *(To the audience)* I tried to explain that this wasn't art.

DAMON. *(To the audience)* Katelyn calls me and says she has a plan. Something surprising, something with Andy. She wants me to make sure he doesn't leave the apartment. Of course I agree to help her.

KATELYN. *(To the audience)* And besides, he's not the only one here who can do something unexpected. So I invite Pamela Sweeney over for dinner and I make Andy the art.

(We hear the sound of a doorbell, the audience has now become the art critic… that is Pamela Sweeney.)

ANDY. *(Extremely upset, flustered)* Katelyn, what are you doing? I'm sorry, Ms. Sweeney, this wasn't discussed.

KATELYN. *(Presenting him to Ms. Sweeney as she might any other piece in her collection)* I realize this seems odd Ms. Sweeney, but I would ask you to consider this carefully. A mutation of pop art, an evolution of conceptualism. I would ask you to consider the ready-made.

(Points to ANDY's face)

We can make a critical statement about the culture we live in. The fact that our bodies have been reduced to ad space.

ANDY. There is nothing here, Katelyn.

DAMON. *(Obviously amused at this plan)* There is definitely something here. A certain…profundity in what Katelyn sees.

ANDY. I wish you'd stop with the word of the day toilet paper. Why are you even here?

DAMON. I warned you about talent man, and this is a talented idea.

ANDY. It's a tattoo. Not art.

KATELYN. How can art exist with the way advertising has intruded into every facet of our daily lives?

DAMON. I can't even get online anymore with all the pop-ups.

ANDY. Then stop going to porn sites.

DAMON. Even before the porn.

ANDY. Give me a break. This is meaningless. Ms. Sweeney, there is a misunderstanding. I'm a person, not art. You seem rather intelligent and I'm sure you noticed.

KATELYN. …THE aesthetic of consumerism.

DAMON. The body as billboard.

ANDY. Go home Damon.

(to KATELYN*)*

We have to start locking the door.

DAMON. I have a key.

KATELYN. Ms. Sweeney, people wear logos all over their clothes, are paid to advertise on their cars. Product placement throughout our movies, a third of our television shows are commercials. Van Gogh's Starry Night has become more associated with credit cards than painting. Mona Lisa's smile eggs us on to buy cameras. Advertising has become our art. This only differs in degree.

ANDY. I am not my portrait! Look Ms. Sweeney…

DAMON. …WE ARE NO longer even portraits of ourselves.

ANDY. What is that even supposed to mean? Okay, I get it. You're having fun with me. This is just a joke, Ms. Sweeney.

KATELYN. This isn't a joke.

ANDY. Just show her the real portrait! I am not it.

KATELYN. This is only the next logical step. The canvas is his skin. Don't you just want to touch it?

ANDY. My skin is not a canvas. I'm getting the real portrait.

(Stands up)

KATELYN. *(With a new seriousness)* Andy, sit down. You have a tattoo on your forehead! People with tattoos on their foreheads don't get to talk right now. They get to listen. So everyone with a tattoo on their forehead sit down and listen.

(He does so after a moment)

This is what we have done to the human body.

DAMON. Walking billboards. Our zeitgeist.

ANDY. If anything can be art then art is dead.

KATELYN. And what do you think killed it?

ANDY. This is dishonest, Katelyn.

KATELYN. As Picasso said, art is a lie that helps us discover the truth.

*(She puts the frame back around **ANDY**'s head, he is frozen. **DAMON** and **KATELYN** step back and look at him as if considering a portrait. After a beat:)*

KATELYN. I knew you would be interested Ms. Sweeney.

Scene 2

(ANDY and KATELYN in the apartment. KATELYN is taking pictures of ANDY with the camera in ACT ONE. ANDY is starting to visibly come undone. He is less sure of himself and has developed a small twitch or other nervous habit. At times he covers the tattoo from the camera with his hands.)

ANDY. You didn't even tell me you were going to do this.

KATELYN. That sounds familiar.

ANDY. Okay, that's fair. But I did this for you too.

KATELYN. Then prove it. This is an opportunity here, Andy. An opportunity for me to prove myself as an artist and for you to prove yourself to me. You said you did it for me...

ANDY. ...I DID DO IT for you, Katelyn.

KATELYN. ...BUT I haven't seen any of the benefits. So I made my own.

(Takes his picture)

ANDY. You didn't create this.

KATELYN. Art is whatever the artist says it is. And I see something artistic here.

(Takes his picture)

ANDY. Can we just talk about this? Without the camera.

KATELYN. I'm documenting you.

ANDY. Do you really expect me to stand on some stage while you talk nonsense about art?

KATELYN. Pamela and I agreed on it.

ANDY. You're not being fair. Katelyn. Listen. I know you're mad. I understand.

KATELYN. I'm not mad Andy.

ANDY. Does this have something to do with your father? Are you trying to prove something to yourself since he was successful?

KATELYN. This has nothing to do with my father.

ANDY. Well I told you why I did it. We haven't talked about that.

KATELYN. I've always thought it was important to remain somewhat detached from the subject. Emotionally speaking.

ANDY. But you don't even care that I got the tattoo anymore. Now I'm just a project. Is that how you're going to relate to me now?

KATELYN. You're the one who objectified yourself.

ANDY. You sold me like a used car!

KATELYN. It was business. You should understand that.

(Mockingly)

I was thinking of our future. I have the Excel sheets if you want to see them.

ANDY. I was humiliated Katelyn.

KATELYN. You said you didn't want me to show the painting.

ANDY. Okay, that was stupid of me. I was being childish. But I take it all back. I like the painting. You should put it in the show. I'll let you.

KATELYN. I'm glad I have your permission but we've already decided on you. You won't change my mind.

(A beat)

ANDY. I got the check yesterday.

(A beat)

KATELYN. And you haven't cashed it yet?

ANDY. It's on the desk. I was waiting.

KATELYN. For what?

ANDY. I don't know.

KATELYN. A higher offer?

ANDY. Just waiting.

KATELYN. Well I thought you would have just run to the bank.

(She takes his picture)

That'll be a good one.

ANDY. I'm trying to talk to you here! I admit, I messed up. I should have discussed this with you before I did it.

KATELYN. It's your body. You're free to do what you want with it.

ANDY. I just want us to be like we were before.

KATELYN. And I want you to have to look at yourself. I want you to see people seeing you. Looking at you like you're a portrait. You're lucky, Andy. You're lucky I see art in this because that's the only thing keeping me here.

ANDY. Can you at least tell me something about what I said the other day. About why I did it. You've been avoiding it.

KATELYN. How could I possibly marry you with that thing on your forehead. Imagine our wedding pictures.

(Takes his picture)

ANDY. Fine. I'm going out for beer.

(He puts on a hat)

KATELYN. Wearing hats now?

(She takes his picture as ANDY *exits.* KATELYN *goes over to the desk, looks for the check and finds it.)*

Scene 3

(**ANDY** *and* **DAMON** *in the apartment drinking beer.*
They have obviously had a lot to drink. It is even more
cluttered than before. Black and white pictures of **ANDY**
at a variety of locations now hang all around the apart-
ment. They are unavoidable.)

ANDY. Pamela Sweeney loved the idea. She even wants Katelyn to do a photo documentary on me. Pictures of me
taking a shower, eating at McDonalds, running. How
the hell could you have helped her do this?

DAMON. Art means a lot to people, Andy. It helps people.

ANDY. And how will this help me?

DAMON. It'll help Katelyn. You don't want to help her?

ANDY. Of course I want to help her. That's why I got the
tattoo.

DAMON. And it's helping her.

ANDY. Yeah, but I didn't want to help her like this.

DAMON. And she didn't want to be helped like this.

ANDY. How come the one time you decide to support Katelyn's career is the one time it makes me look like an
ass?

DAMON. I'm not doing anything to make you look like an
ass.

ANDY. I went to get food the other night and I swear everyone was laughing at me. How the hell can I stand on a
stage? No way.

DAMON. Rock and a hard place man. That's what they say.

ANDY. No thanks to you. Why does this kind of shit always
happen to me?

DAMON. We all got problems man.

ANDY. And what problems could you possibly have?

DAMON. Global warming.

ANDY. Don't start on this shit now.

DAMON. That's a major fucking crisis right there. Think
about that.

ANDY. Oh Jesus.

DAMON. Jesus isn't doing anything about it. Just look at Mount Kilimanjaro.

ANDY. What about it?

DAMON. Snow-covered peaks for tens of thousands of years and now just puddles and mud. And to think the government says we need more research. All we need to do is take a look at Mount Kilimanjaro and we'll see the effects of global warming.

ANDY. You should protest the sun.

DAMON. Don't patronize me. It's a serious epidemic, Andy.

ANDY. Well I don't see what we can do about it. The world's going to burn up anyway. Besides, who goes to the top of Mount Kilimanjaro?

DAMON. That's a great attitude Andy. That's your problem.

ANDY. What?

DAMON. You have a bad attitude. Like Richard Nixon bad.

ANDY. ...Please...I don't need this today. Besides, you're the one who sold me.

DAMON. ...You never need anything any day...except a better attitude and a new forehead.

ANDY. My attitude is fine. I don't need a better attitude. I need friends who don't plot to sell me.

DAMON. Fine, fine. But don't come crying to me when you have skin cancer.

ANDY. Why would I go crying to you if I had skin cancer? I'd go to a doctor.

DAMON. People do odd things when faced with their mortality, Andy. So don't come running to me.

ANDY. I won't.

DAMON. Good. God damn Charles Manson.

ANDY. Fucking ridiculous. Selling me.

(**ANDY** *pushes him hard and* **DAMON** *pushes him back and then runs away*)

Don't push me, you pacifist.

(He starts after him, almost cartoonishly. They've had, after all, a lot to drink)

DAMON. Leave me alone. Ozone hater.

ANDY. Nader Rader.

(Pushes him down)

Now take it back.

DAMON. What?

ANDY. Tell me I don't have an attitude problem because I don't sell my friends

DAMON. Never.

ANDY. *(Puts more weight on him, hurting him)* Tell me.

DAMON. *(Struggling)* Fine. Fine. You have a beautiful attitude. The best attitude. If there was an award for attitudes they'd give it to you only they wouldn't bother because they'd know your attitude is so humble yet amazingly good that you'd just give the award to someone else.

ANDY. And my forehead?

DAMON. I love your forehead. I wish it was my forehead.

ANDY. You don't mean it.

DAMON. I do! I swear!

ANDY. I don't believe you.

DAMON. *(Looking at the tattoo)* Holy shit! Your tattoo!

ANDY. *(Gets off of him quickly, touching his forehead)* What?

DAMON. It's glowing… the tattoo.

ANDY. What are you talking about?

DAMON. It was glowing.

ANDY. You're full of shit.

DAMON. I swear to god.

ANDY. You're seeing things.

(He runs to the mirror and checks out the tattoo)

DAMON. It was glowing. Like lights. Bright lights.

ANDY. You were just trying to get me off of you.

DAMON. I swear man. It was neon.

ANDY. You're seeing shit. That's all.

DAMON. Neon billboard.

ANDY. Look at it…

DAMON. …Glowing like a superhero.

ANDY. …It's not glowing.

DAMON. But it was.

ANDY. …You're drunk.

DAMON. Yeah but you were glowing man. Like some corporate asshole superhero.

ANDY. I'm not a superhero…

DAMON. Glowing Tattoo Man. They probably used some special ink. Something toxic. Most likely the government running tests on you.

ANDY. IT WASN'T GLOWING!

DAMON. Whatever man.

ANDY. So stop looking at it!

DAMON. Calm down, I was just messing with you. Man, you're really stressed out. Drink another beer.

(They sit back down on the couch and open another round of beers, there is a long silence)

DAMON. Think you guys will break up?

ANDY. We're not going to break up.

DAMON. I hope not man. I'd be a wreck.

ANDY. Thanks for the concern. She's just trying to make a point.

DAMON. I don't know man. She's pretty into it.

ANDY. It's a joke.

DAMON. Not to her. Hey, you wanna know something?

ANDY. No.

DAMON. There are more obese people in the world now than starving people. Think about that.

(Silence)

ANDY. Questa.

(silence)

DAMON. Fucking Questa.

ANDY. Questa.

DAMON. You remember that whole Christo and Jean-Claude thing they did in Central Park? I remember when they were showing it on the news and I saw this homeless guy in the background just staring up at one of the flags. Man he must have been wondering how they could spend so much money to decorate a park full of homeless people. Sure, covering Central Park in orange curtains may be great and beautiful and all that, but man, what if they had used those millions of dollars to buy every homeless person in New York brilliant orange suits? Then everyone would know who was homeless from blocks away and could take them out to eat. No one would be afraid to take them to a restaurant because the homeless would be the best dressed people in the city.

You know what we should do? We should go cash that check and buy suits. Fucking Armani. Then we'll go to the nicest, most expensive bar we can find in this city. And we'll go up to hottest girl we can find and we'll buy her a drink. The fanciest stuff they have. And we'll just sit there and talk to her. Classy. And then we'll thank her and say good night and drive to the nastiest, diviest bar we can find. And we'll go up to the dirtiest, ugliest woman we can find and buy her a shot of cheap whiskey. And we'll talk to her. Then we'll say good night to her. That's what we should do. In Armani suits.

(Long pause)

ANDY. Maybe that homeless guy was thinking how beautiful it was.

DAMON. Maybe.

(Long pause)

ANDY. God damn Questa.

DAMON. Questa, fucking Questa.

ANDY. Questa.

DAMON. Ques-ta.

ANDY. Qu-es-ta.

DAMON. Qu

ANDY. Es

DAMON. Ta

Scene 4

(**ANDY**, *alone to the audience*)

ANDY. After I fell asleep it started itching. It felt like there were ants all over my face. Then it started growing and stretching. First, covering my head. Then my chest and before long my whole body was covered. Not one inch of my skin showed through. And I felt a certain relief that I was no longer myself. No one would ever see me for who I am again. Then Katelyn appeared.

(**KATELYN** *appears*)

And she said:

KATELYN. Andy, I'm pregnant.

ANDY. And we were so happy. Surprised but happy. And her belly grew big.

(*Her belly grows*)

And she said:

KATELYN. Andy, my water broke.

(*Her water breaks*)

ANDY. (*To* **KATELYN**) Hurry, get in the bed.

(*She gets in the bed*)

She got in bed and I delivered the baby.

(*He delivers the baby, we hear all the sounds associated with pregnancy*)

It was an easy pregnancy and I somehow knew what I was doing, but it wasn't a baby at all. It was something small and hard. It was an iPod. She gave birth to an iPod. And instead of cutting the umbilical cord I cut the power cord.

(*He pulls out a bloody iPod as if she had given birth to it,* **KATELYN** *screams and then lays back exhausted*)

She was mad and yelled:

KATELYN. You can't even give me a real child!

ANDY. I felt suspicious that she didn't give birth to a Questa product. Like I wasn't the father or something. And then I noticed that music was coming from it.

(He holds it to his ear.)

Faintly. The Beatles. Magical Mystery Tour.
When I woke up alone, I immediately checked the tattoo but it had shrunk back to it's normal size.

Scene 5

(KATELYN and ANDY sit on opposite ends of the couch. ANDY is practicing his Saxophone. He is horrible. KATELYN is watching television. The television plays loudly. ANDY plays loudly. KATELYN looks only straight ahead at the television. ANDY is now near manic. He is extremely nervous and flustered.)

ANDY. *(After a long pause)* What did they say?

KATELYN. What?

ANDY. On the phone. What did they say?

KATELYN. Nothing.

ANDY. They said something.

KATELYN. I don't remember.

ANDY. You just hung up like a minute ago.

KATELYN. It was nothing. Do you have to keep blowing that thing?

(He stops for a moment and then blows again.)

KATELYN. I'm trying to watch TV.

ANDY. I used to be good. Talented enough to be in a band.

KATELYN. I can tell.

(He sets the saxophone down)

ANDY. So you talked nearly an hour.

KATELYN. They were just asking me some questions.

ANDY. An interview?

KATELYN. About the art show.

(Pause)

ANDY. I thought they were calling for me. An interview about the tattoo.

KATELYN. No.

ANDY. When I picked up the phone and they said who it was I was sure it was for me.

KATELYN. Nope. Are you okay?

ANDY. I'm fine. Why?

KATELYN. You're acting funny.

ANDY. That's great. That they wanted to talk to you.

KATELYN. Yeah. Are you sure you're okay, Andy?

ANDY. So what did you say?

KATELYN. I talked about my work.

ANDY. Did you talk about me?

KATELYN. A little.

ANDY. I am your work after all.

KATELYN. Not exactly.

ANDY. What did they think when you told them?

KATELYN. They thought it was interesting.

ANDY. Were they interested in me at all? Other than as art.

KATELYN. The interviewer was an art critic.

ANDY. Didn't he think it was odd that you were using a real person?

KATELYN. It's common.

ANDY. Well I'm happy for you.

(Pause, they watch television)

KATELYN. I'm tired. I'm going to bed.

(She gets up)

ANDY. What if I got it removed now? With lasers? I can break the contract as long as we don't cash the check.

KATELYN. *(After a pause)* You'll never be able to remove it completely.

(She exits into the bedroom. ANDY continues to watch television for a few moments. A Questa commercial comes on the television. ANDY picks up the remote control and tries to shut it off but it only gets louder. The stage is covered in a projection of the Questa logo.)

COMMERCIAL. *(Over music, with all the sounds and chaos of a commerical)* When it comes to music and video technology there is only one name to trust. Questa. Sound so clear you'd swear you were at the concert. Pictures so clear you'd swear you were at the game. Questa. The sound you've been searching for. Questa.

ANDY. Oh Jesus. Damn batteries! Katelyn, where are the batteries?

KATELYN. *(Off stage)* In the closet.

(He goes over and opens the closet to get new batteries. The portrait falls out. He picks it up and stares at it for a moment, with the audience unable to fully make it out, especially in the light.)

ANDY. Katelyn! Get in here. Katelyn!

*(**KATELYN** enters while in the process of getting ready for bed)*

KATELYN. What?

ANDY. Where's the tattoo?!

KATELYN. Why are you yelling?!

ANDY. When did you paint over this?

KATELYN. Calm down. What are you talking about?

ANDY. I didn't know you painted over the tattoo.

KATELYN. I didn't paint over anything.

ANDY. *(Holding up the painting)* The tattoo is gone. It's not on my face anymore.

KATELYN. There was never a tattoo on your face.

ANDY. Of course there was. You painted me with the tattoo. It was there.

KATELYN. No I didn't. I painted you the way I prefer you. Why would I paint you with the tattoo? I hate the tattoo.

ANDY. *(Remembering, doubting himself)* It was there. In paint.

KATELYN. *(Now bewildered)* It was never there Andy.

ANDY. Of course it was.

KATELYN. No.

ANDY. *(Desperate)* Promise me.

KATELYN. I promise.

ANDY. You mean…all this…Jesus Christ…Katelyn…what

did I do to myself?
You were right.

(He looks at the painting)

I'm sorry, Katelyn.
This is good.

Scene 6

(KATELYN and DAMON in the apartment. The painting is back on the easel, unseen by the audience. DAMON is looking closely at the painting.)

DAMON. I'm no doctor but that can't be good.

KATELYN. He's been asleep all day.

DAMON. There's a small freckle, a dot, but nothing that could even come close to passing for the tattoo.

KATELYN. That's what he saw.

DAMON. I don't know.

(Pause)

Maybe he should see a doctor.

KATELYN. I don't know what to do.

DAMON. And how are you? Okay?

KATELYN. I guess so. Busy. The show.

DAMON. It's a great idea. You really have talent, Katelyn.

KATELYN. Thanks. Maybe it was too far though.

DAMON. He went too far when he got the tattoo. We were just catching up.

KATELYN. I have to have him there.

DAMON. I'll be there. And I'm sure Andy will be too. You know the monkeys that took care of the goldfish and didn't let them die did better on the puzzles. They were smarter. Almost all of them were female.

KATELYN. I think you're right.

DAMON. You know about the monkey-goldfish experiments?!

KATELYN. No. But for some reason that just made sense.

(Enter ANDY looking like hell. He is tired, unkempt, and in a daze.)

DAMON. You look like hell man.

ANDY. Did you move in or something?

DAMON. Katelyn called me. Are you okay? She said you freaked out.

ANDY. I'm ripping up the check and getting it removed. I can't live a whole year like this.

DAMON. Good choice man.

ANDY. You were both right so you don't have to say you told me so. I would have never thought it could affect me on the level it did. I didn't even know I had another level.

DAMON. None of us did, Andy.

KATELYN. Are you sure you want to do that? I mean, you signed a contract after all.

ANDY. It doesn't matter, I never cashed the check. If I rip up the check they can't do anything.

KATELYN. I think you should think about it.

ANDY. That's too much thinking. I saw things that weren't there. I don't need to think about anything.

KATELYN. At least wait a day or two to be sure. You haven't been yourself.

ANDY. Exactly. I thought you'd be thrilled I'm getting it removed.

KATELYN. I am. It's just…

ANDY. …The art show. I'm sorry Katelyn but I can't. It's too much for me. It's a good idea but it was your idea, not mine. You know it's not my thing.

KATELYN. All you would have to do is stand there and move a little. That's it.

ANDY. While people stare at me like I'm in a zoo.

KATELYN. I can't just pull a piece days before a show, Andy. Especially a show like this.

ANDY. I'm sorry, but I never said I would do it.

DAMON. You know who was an artist? Hitler. Before the war.

ANDY. I've heard that.

DAMON. Can you imagine if you owned a Hitler? Here's my Picasso and my Monet, but here is my Hitler. A piece from his green period, before he killed 6 million people.

KATELYN. *(Becoming visibly flustered, upset)* You can't just be getting tattoos one day and getting them removed the next. How am I supposed to know who you are?

ANDY. You've been saying from the beginning that I should get it removed. You told me so.

KATELYN. Most people put a lot of thought into getting a tattoo but not you.

ANDY. Most people don't think about what tattoo they get. They just get drunk with a bunch of friends and go get something.

DAMON. That's what my Uncle did. He got the number sixteen on his arm. That's how many beers he had before.

KATELYN. This isn't easy, Andy. That money, I thought it was ours.

ANDY. So now you're worried about money, after all the shit you gave me?

DAMON. I bet a Hitler would be worth millions.

KATELYN. I never cared about the money. But things have changed.

ANDY. You're being absurd, Katelyn. What is wrong with you?

KATELYN. Nothing is wrong with me. I didn't do anything.

ANDY. Then tell me what you didn't do.

KATELYN. The money...there was a lot.

ANDY. Yes, a lot of money you don't care about.

KATELYN. Yes, but you're not understanding.

ANDY. Then tell me.

KATELYN. All of this, the pictures, the construction, the painting...putting this installation together has cost a lot of money.

ANDY. *(Really noticing all of the pictures and art supplies that crowd the small apartment for the first time)*
We'll make up for it...

KATELYN. ...MONEY we didn't have without the check.

(A beat. Andy goes over to the desk and looks for the

check, tossing papers aside)

ANDY. What are you saying Katelyn? Where is it? Where is the check?! What did you do with the check? The check was here and now it isn't, so where is it, Katelyn?! Where is the check with my name on it?!

DAMON. You cashed the check?

KATELYN. I needed it, Andy.

ANDY. Jesus Christ, Katelyn!

KATELYN. I had to.

ANDY. You sold me off!

KATELYN. You sold yourself! Pamela Sweeney was pressuring me to make this good. I couldn't afford to be cheap. When I told her we had no money coming in she said, "What about all the Questa money?"

ANDY. How?

KATELYN. I took your card and put it in the ATM.

ANDY. JESUS KATELYN, HOW THE HELL COULD YOU HAVE DONE THAT TO ME...

DAMON. ...YOU COULDN'T have spent that much of the money. Just come up with the rest and send it back. I'll help out.

ANDY. How much?

(pause)

KATELYN. About three-thousand.

ANDY. On art?

DAMON. Jesus.

KATELYN. The camera broke. I had to fix it. And all the film and processing. Supplies. I didn't think it would cost so much. It went so fast.

ANDY. And what else did you buy? New clothes? Shoes?

KATELYN. Nothing, Andy.

ANDY. It doesn't matter anyway. Cashing the check was the final confirmation. If I get it removed now we'd have to give all the money back plus a huge fine for breaking the contract.

KATELYN. I'm sorry, Andy, but I thought I was doing what you were going to do anyway.

ANDY. Then you should have let ME do it! I'm going to go crazy now because of you.

DAMON. I think you should do the show, Andy. I think it'll help.

ANDY. Oh great, another idea.

DAMON. It will be like you're turning the tables on Questa. You'll be making a statement.

ANDY. How will standing there like an idiot be making a statement?

DAMON. You'll be reclaiming it. Making it your own. Like the N word.

ANDY. Don't even start on the N word again.

DAMON. No, really Andy. Shove it in people's faces. The tattoo doesn't just make you look like a fool, it makes our whole culture look moronic, that this is what influences people to go and buy more shit.

ANDY. I'm not going to do the show.

KATELYN. Please Andy. Just do the show. I need you. Do you think people get opportunities like this all the time? And after everything I put up with.

ANDY. ...You're the one who stole and cashed the check!

KATELYN. ...BECAUSE this could start my career. Most people, Andy, would have walked out the moment you walked in with the tattoo.

ANDY. It would have been better than this!

KATELYN. You know that isn't true.

(Silence)

DAMON. It's like when a guy missing an eye walks into a bar. You gotta look because you have to know what it looks like to have one eye. But afterwards it's no big deal. Just a guy with one eye who wants a drink.

(Silence)

ANDY. I'm sick of the whole thing. I'm tired of the tattoo, of money, of fighting, of seeing things that aren't there, of not eating together, of brushing my teeth. I am so sick of brushing my teeth and looking in the mirror.

(Silence)

KATELYN. Please Andy, look at what this has done to us. You have a chance to make this into art.

*(**KATELYN** exits after a beat)*

ANDY. Jesus. What the hell am I going to do?

DAMON. Katelyn is the best thing you have going man. I know you, you need somebody. You're not good on your own, especially now that you have all this other shit to deal with. And let's face it, it's not like you're going to meet someone else as long as you have that thing on your head. If you don't do it she might leave you and it's worth saving.

ANDY. She might leave me if I do.

DAMON. You want my advice? Do everything you can to keep her. You're never going to find a better girl.

ANDY. Do you think it would be art?

DAMON. Katelyn is the artist.

ANDY. Yeah, but is that why she's doing this?

DAMON. I don't know.

ANDY. That's a first.

DAMON. She has always wanted to be an artist. Now you can make her one.

ANDY. Maybe.

DAMON. Andy, I never told you this, but at my dad's funeral, Katelyn said the only thing that made me feel any better. And believe me, lots of people said lots of things.

ANDY. What did she say?

DAMON. She said, "My father died, too."

Scene 7

(A memory. **KATELYN** *and* **ANDY** *are in bed. There are no cameras now.)*

ANDY. *(To the audience)* An excerpt continued.

KATELYN. Do you really think we'll last?

ANDY. Even if every house looked exactly the same and so did the people inside, I would still go home to the right house. Know why?

KATELYN. Why?

ANDY. Because you're the one.

KATELYN. You think so?

ANDY. I'm sure of it.

KATELYN. What if I want two?

ANDY. I wouldn't believe you.

KATELYN. And why is that?

ANDY. I'm more than enough man for any woman.

KATELYN. Please.

ANDY. Fine. Since you're such a Salinger expert, remember the end of "The Catcher in the Rye" when Holden can't stop watching his sister on the carousel and it's pouring rain, but he doesn't leave because he says she looks so damn nice going around and around?

KATELYN. I do as matter of fact.

ANDY. Well even if it was pouring rain I'd still sit on the bench and watch you. Even though I couldn't write about it like Salinger after.

(She kisses him)

KATELYN. But I'm not your sister.

ANDY. True. You know, you should paint me sometime. I'd be an incredible model.

(He flexes)

KATELYN. I don't think I'd be able to capture your handsomeness. You need Cezanne.

ANDY. Cezanne rarely painted people.

KATELYN. You're learning.

ANDY. Besides, you're the only person I'd let paint me.

KATELYN. Well at least my boyfriend thinks I'm good.

ANDY. Lots of people do.

KATELYN. People in college. That doesn't count.

ANDY. Sure it does.

KATELYN. College is just doing better than average. You do better than average and you're praised. And the average isn't very high.

ANDY. Maybe. But you're good. I mean it. You just have to do it. You can't worry about money or anything else.

KATELYN. But college is one thing and a career completely different. I don't know if I could really actually do it. Be an artist. You can't even say you're an artist anymore. My father always refused to call himself an artist. He'd get mad every time my mom referred to him as one.

ANDY. I wish I knew your dad.

KATELYN. It's just become a euphemism for unemployed loser. Only people with money can be artists anymore. And rich artists don't even make their own work. They hire poor artists to create their ideas. That's why artists become irrelevant as soon as they make money.

ANDY. Do you really believe that?

KATELYN. Sometimes.

ANDY. I think you have a real shot at making it. Sure, you have to get lucky, but you've got the talent.

KATELYN. It's hard. You have to sell yourself. It's all become so corporate and weird. Like how some of the world's greatest paintings hang in Vegas hotels. I hate that.

ANDY. Who wants to look at art when they're in Vegas?

KATELYN. Yeah, I know what you want to look at.

ANDY. Not even. Of course it's hard but you are so good. If you didn't pursue this it would be a waste. I'll help you out. I'll support you. We'll support each other.

KATELYN. I love you.

(She kisses him.)

ANDY. I love you too.

Scene 8

(ANDY and KATELYN in the apartment. KATELYN lays out a suit for ANDY. She is preparing to leave, looking at herself in the mirror, fixing her hair, applying last touches of make-up, etc. ANDY sits on the couch watching her. KATELYN then gets some materials together, papers and so forth, as well as a packed bag, and heads for the door. She stops and looks at ANDY. There is a long silence before ANDY speaks.)

ANDY. What are you going to do?

KATELYN. I don't know. I'll tell them my exhibit refused to come.

ANDY. *(Placating)* Very post-modern.

(Silence)

Remember when we listened to all the Beatles albums?

KATELYN. Of course I remember. It meant everything to me.

ANDY. It rained the entire day.

KATELYN. I still say Magical Mystery Tour.

ANDY. No way, Abbey Road.

(Long silence, KATELYN begins to leave again, ANDY notices the bag.)

ANDY. What's that?

KATELYN. My bag.

ANDY. What's in it?

KATELYN. My clothes.

ANDY. Aren't you coming home tonight?

KATELYN. I don't know.

(She leaves. ANDY sits there for a long time in silence. He then goes over to the suit. After a moment he begins to put it on.)

Scene 9

(**ANDY** *is now in the gallery. Several lights shine from the ground up at him. One light focuses on the tattoo.*)

ANDY. *(Alone, to the audience)* One day at the Getty, Katelyn got mad at me because I refused to admit that the giant, chaotic, splashy Pollock deserved to hang next to, or even in the same room, as the Monet. I'll admit, there is something to the Pollock. There is emotion and maybe, somewhere in all of the drippings and splattering, maybe there is even something being communicated. As Damon says, I'm no art critic, but I couldn't see how it could justly hang next to Monet's "Cathedral in Morning Light," a painting which changes with every step. From thirty feet a detailed masterpiece. Photographic even. But from one foot a screen of monochromatic paint camouflaging the treasure within. A painting I couldn't do on the floor of a garage.

Katelyn went off on the end of art. The act of painting as the metaphor. Art in response to photography and war. Art in the face of consumerism. But at the end of the day it is paint splashed on a canvas, nothing more.

One day we'll go to the museum and all that will be hanging on the walls will be cans of paint. The symbolism is seething.

It's like Damon's whole Christo and Jean-Claude thing. I agree it's a stupid and sophomoric idea, but at the same time, he has a point. Was that homeless guy thinking "this is beautiful" or "this is waste?"

I guess that's his talent, saying stupid things that somehow, in the end, have a certain...profundity.

And Katelyn's talent? Seeing art. I saw money and she saw art and maybe that's the only thing that separates everyone in the world.

But after it was all said and done I had to give her something. And she was able to take something she hated and make it entirely her own.

I guess that's why Christo and Jean-Claude do what they do. It's their way of understanding the world. Of making it their own in a way.

The response to Katelyn's work has been positive. She's being talked about. There's discussion of future work. And the painting? Well the painting will serve as a reminder for me because soon it will all be gone. The interviews, the tattoo, the art, the dreams, the money...

But we'll be fine. Because before I left it alone I took one long, deep look at the Pollock and the art spoke to me. For a moment, in the chaotic splash of color, I saw Katelyn and it was the most beautiful painting in the museum. In any museum. And I knew it was good. There was none of this other shit that blinds us from the art of it all. That distorts how we see things. Because really, in the end, we're all standing in front of the same canvas, squinting our eyes, trying to figure out what the hell it means. Hoping to see something we recognize.

(Blackout.)

End of Play

OTHER TITLES AVAILABLE FROM SAMUEL FRENCH

JACK GOES BOATING
Bob Glaudini

Full Length / Comedy / 2m, 2f / Interior
Four flawed but likeable lower-middle-class New Yorkers interact in a touching and warmhearted play about learning how to stay afloat in the deep water of day-to-day living. Laced with cooking classes, swimming lessons and a smorgasbord of illegal drugs, *Jack Goes Boating* is a story of date panic, marital meltdown, betrayal, and the prevailing grace of the human spirit.

"An immensely likable play [that] exudes a wry compassion."
- *The New York Times*

"Endearing romantic comedy about a married couple and the social-misfit friends they fix up. Witty and knowing and all heart."
- *Variety*

"Glides effortlessly from the shallow end of the emotional pool to the deep end."
- *Theatremania.com*